TIGERS

by Roland Edwards
pictures by Judith Riches

Tambourine Books New York

There are tigers on the landing
right outside my bedroom door.
I know they're prowling up and down,
soft footsteps on the floor.

They're very, very quiet
and they're very, very shy.
They never tiger talk at all
as they go padding by.

You will never see a tiger
steal across the floor.
But if you're very quiet,
you might hear a whispered roar.

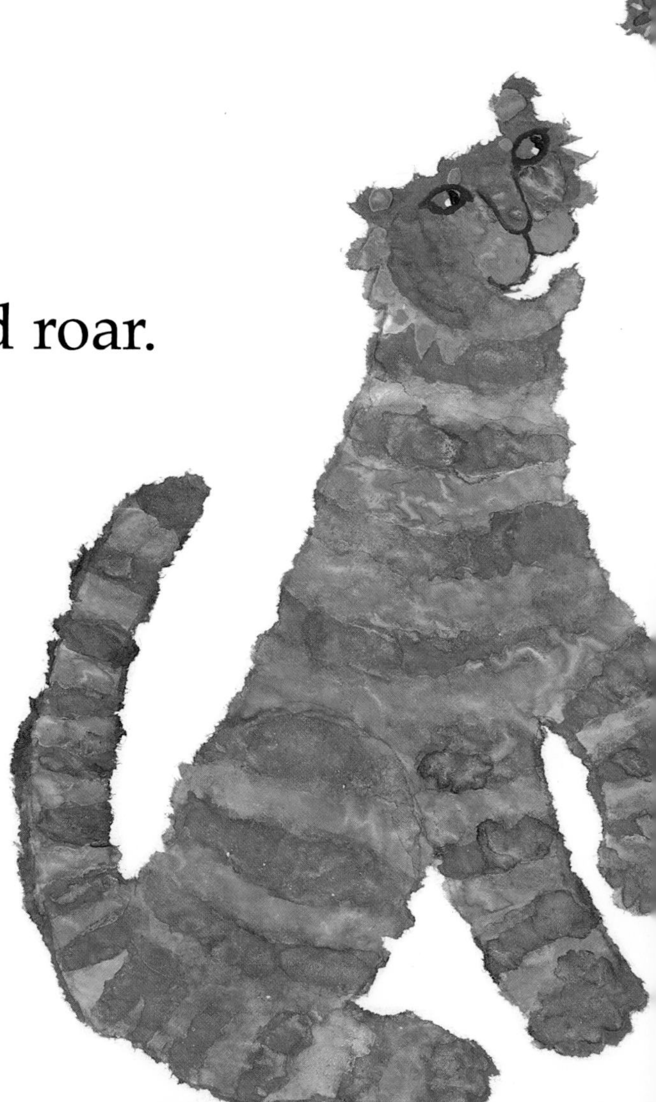

There are some up in the attic,
I think maybe three or four.
I hear them scuffle round,
but I really can't keep score.

They play a special game up there.
It's called Big Cats and Mice.
In silence circling softly,
though I've heard them once or twice.

And nobody gets hurt
as they lope around the floor.
But each time one is caught,
I can hear a whispered roar.

There's a tiger
in the cupboard
with the single
broken drawer,
in the room that
Mommy goes to
so she can't hear
Daddy snore.

The tiger lives there by himself,
it really is a shame.
I know he might be lonely,
but he's happy, all the same.
He hunts the cupboard spiders,
he's always finding more.
And every time he captures one,
he gives a whispered roar.

And outside on the rooftop,
I think more tigers play.
They chase each other's tails about,
but never seem to stray.

They crawl up to the very top
and slide down on their backs.
And in the winter, when it's snowing,
you can see their slidey tracks.

They play long games
of hide-and-seek
round chimneys
and the door.
And when they find
each other, they give
a whispered roar.

But Daddy says, don't worry,
as he tucks me in real tight.
It's just the heating murmuring
and whispering at night.

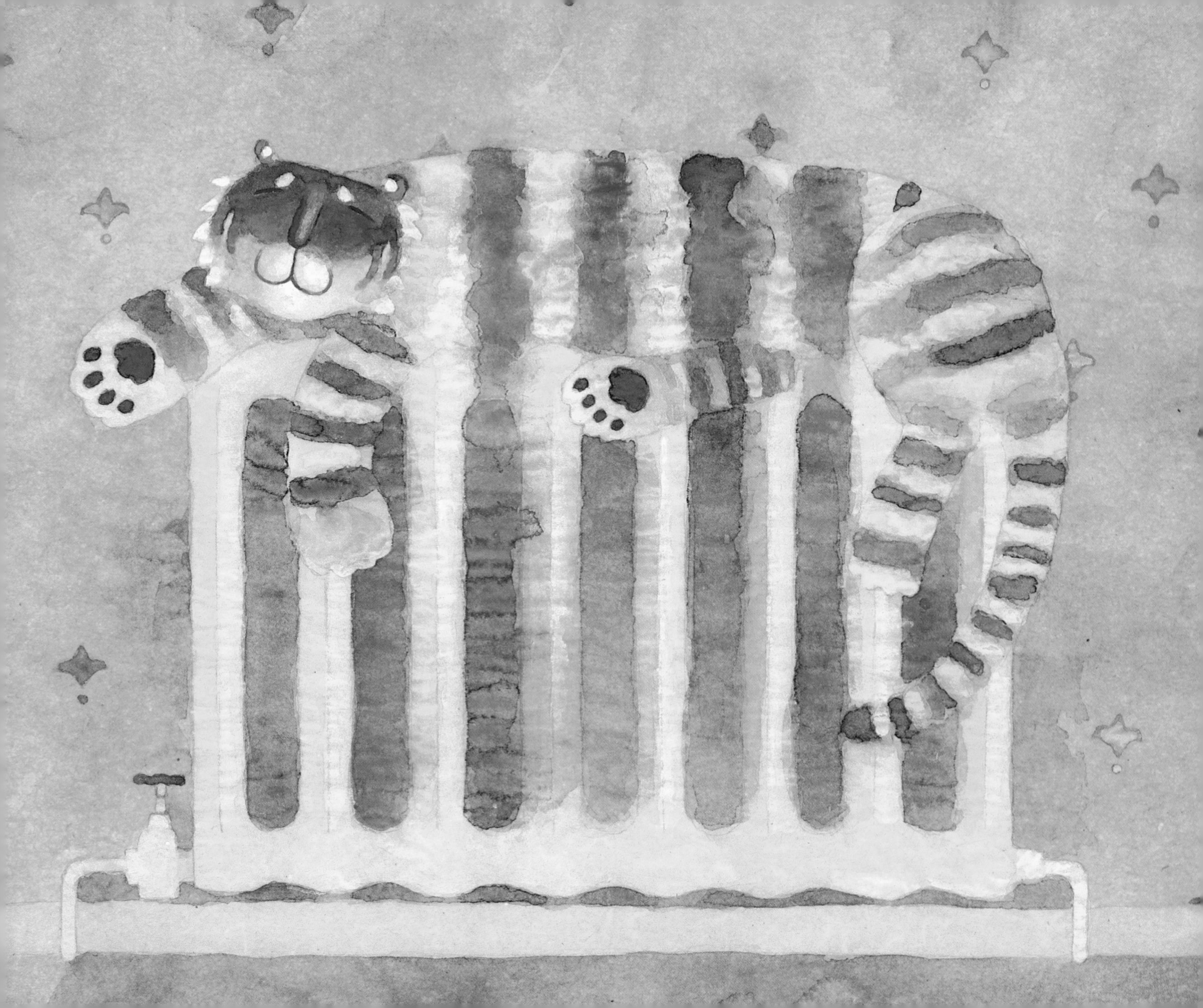

E EDW
Edwards, Roland
Tigers /
33910031351019 gp
$15.00 06/04/99
DISCARD

Garfield Park Activity Center
26 Karlyn Drive
New Castle, DE 19720
DISCARD